FRIENDS
OF ACPL

W9-DIG-977

GIB MORGAN
Oil Driller

OTHER BOOKS BY HAROLD W. FELTON

Legends of Paul Bunyan
Pecos Bill: Texas Cowpuncher
John Henry and His Hammer
Fire-Fightin' Mose
Bowleg Bill: Seagoing Cowpuncher
Cowboy Jamboree: Western Songs and Lore
New Tall Tales of Pecos Bill
Mike Fink: Best of the Keelboatmen
A Horse Named Justin Morgan
Sergeant O'Keefe and His Mule, Balaam
Pecos Bill and the Mustang
Jim Beckwourth, Negro Mountain Man
Edward Rose, Negro Trail Blazer
True Tall Tales of Stormalong
Nat Love, Negro Cowboy
Mumbet: The Story of Elizabeth Freeman
James Weldon Johnson

GIB MORGAN

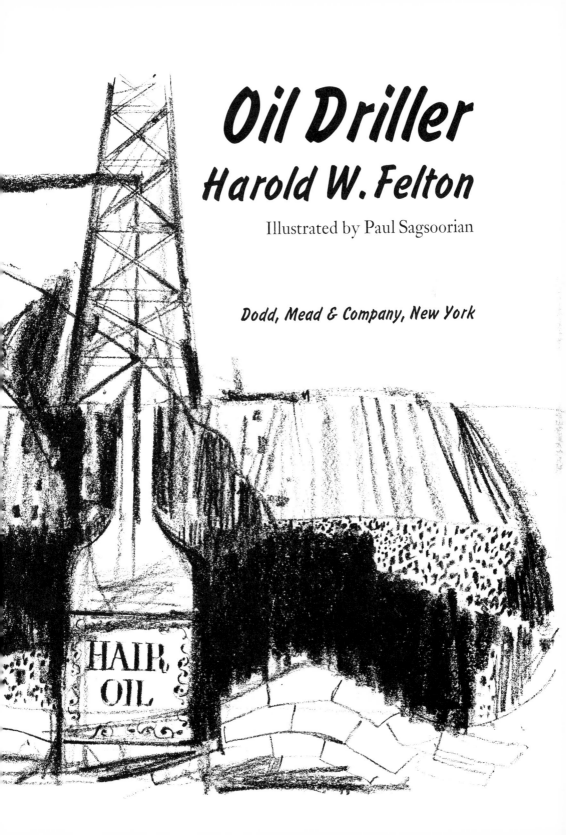

Oil Driller
Harold W. Felton

Illustrated by Paul Sagsoorian

Dodd, Mead & Company, New York

HAIR
OIL

To Arthur

Copyright © 1972 by University of Nebraska Foundation
All rights reserved
No part of this book may be reproduced in any form
without permission in writing from the publisher
ISBN: 0-396-06583-X
Library of Congress Catalog Card Number: 72-1535
Printed in the United States of America

CO. SCHOOLS
C850730

Contents

Introduction

THE FACTS OF Gib Morgan's life and the tales he told have been assembled by Professor Mody C. Boatright in a book published by the Texas Folk-Lore Society in 1945. His work was made possible by grants in aid from the Research Institute of the University of Texas and, through the Texas State Historical Association, from the Rockefeller Foundation. His book is called *Gib Morgan, Minstrel of the Oil Fields.*

Professor Boatright states that he did not attempt to set down the tales verbatim. He calls attention to one of the realities of yarn spinning, the possibility of infinite variation. And he points out that Gib Morgan "never told a tale in the same way twice." I too have made choices of emphasis and selection.

Gib Morgan was an oil driller, and the point of his drill found the stuff that made empires. Born in Callensburg, Clarion county, in western Pennsylvania on July 14, 1842, he moved with his parents, while still a boy, to nearby Alum Rock and then to Emlenton in Venango county. The name they wrote

9

down in the family Bible was Gilbert. His father was a farmer,
a lumberman, a raftsman, a builder of barges, and a man who
was able to construct his own house. Gib had seven brothers
and sisters.

On August 27, 1859, when Gib was seventeen years old, a
great event occurred in Titusville, only forty miles away. Uncle
Billy Smith, working for Colonel Edwin L. Drake, struck oil.
Gib Morgan saw the well, smelled the oil, and caught the oil
fever that sped through the land. He saw the fortune seekers
who rushed to grasp for the wealth that could be found in the
ground. He saw his first oil well fire. The driller struck a gas
pocket. There was an explosion, searing flame. And nineteen
men died.

Gib heard of the firing on Fort Sumter that took place on
April 12, 1861, and enlisted on April 25, giving his age as
twenty-one years, thus telling the only lie he ever told for the
purpose of deceiving.

He fought in two fistfuls of battles with the Venango Greys
of the Tenth Pennsylvania Regiment. He returned home in
June, 1864, and soon became an oil man. An oil man he
remained.

It is not difficult to find tall tales in the oil industry. Not
the kind Gib Morgan told, but those that come from the efforts
of geologists, chemists, engineers, industrialists. Almost over-
night the magic of oil—black gold—turned the poor farmer or
workman into a business tycoon or industrial giant. The story
of the wildcatter is not unusual. In debt over his head, dis-

couraged, with the last shred of hope gone, with optimism all but drained from him, suddenly he is transformed into a modern Croesus by the roar and rush of oil.

Petroleum, that clearly ought to be pumped from a well, sometimes is not. Tall tale-like, it often gushes high in the air. And it may require more energy and technical skill to keep it in the ground than it does to get it out.

The finding, the digging, the production of petroleum are never-ending tall tales. Pipe lines lace the land, the primeval goo is changed into liquids, solids, and gas, and these, in turn, are changed into goodness knows how many useful products. Petroleum, sought in the first instance to supply fuel for lamps, has been searched for as the rainbow's end in every country and in every ocean. It is now used for the production of drugs and plastics, and in innumerable items from paving material to paint, from soap to cattle feed. There seems to be no limit to the magic of chemistry when it approaches the combination of carbon and hydrogen molecules of the stuff Gib Morgan yarned about, sought, and found.

Our tall tale heroes have commonly been involved in work. For the most part, they were the masters of the simple tools of another age. Paul Bunyan reached his fame with an axe and an ox; Pecos Bill with a rope and a horse; John Henry with a hammer; Mike Fink with a pole and an oar; Big Mose, the volunteer fireman, with a ladder and a water hose.

But here is something new: the complications of finance, geology, and machines. Gib worked in a more complicated arena, the world of derricks and rigs, of pulleys and cables, of Samson posts and walking beams. He made his mark with a string of tools—the tools needed to locate and bring to the surface the fabulous black gold. If his tales were tall, the truth was not far behind.

Gib Morgan's tales were told at the dawn of our industrial age, and tall tale characters will continue to appear, one may be sure. It will be interesting for a future generation to see the emergence of those who will deal with digital computers, cryogenics, thermodynamics, nuclear power, and the like. But still, it is possible to wonder how tall yarns will develop out of such tall tale facts.

In the early oil fields, the driller was the boss. Frederick A. Talbot in *The Oil Conquest of the World* points out: "The expert driller is of a class apart—self-reliant, enterprising, persevering, optimistic, and of uncanny resource. . . . The driller . . . depends upon his own observations and the 'feel' of the tools as they are working . . . able to detect by sound and touch the slightest deviation from the normal rhythm of his charge."

Gib was a driller, but more than that, he was a yarn spinner, a tall tale teller. Things happened to Gib Morgan—strange things that rarely, if ever, happened to anyone else—and he told about them. If it might seem to some that they couldn't have happened, he made it sound as though they did. He told his yarns, and they stayed told. Only the best tall tale tellers can tell them that well.

HAROLD W. FELTON

1

Gib Morgan's Oil Poultice

THERE WAS a giant groan. The steam engine's wheels and belts shuddered and strained and then stopped cold.

"What's wrong here?" asked Gib Morgan. "We've got a good head of steam."

"The engine's workin' fine," said Little Toolie. "You fixed her up real good." He tossed a few chunks of wood on the hungry fire. "When it comes to handlin' machines, it seems like you are able to think with your hands."

It was the second oil-drilling rig ever built, or the third. Maybe the fourth. At any rate, it was an early one. Uncle Billy Smith built the first one over in Titusville, Pennsylvania, not far from Gib's boyhood home.

Gib Morgan, at the age of seventeen, had taken one look at Uncle Billy's rig. He had heard the creak and groan of the pumps, the squeak and rumble of the pulleys, and the puffing of the steam engine. He saw the mud and the water. He smelled the oil. At once he decided to become an oil driller and sink his own well.

He built a derrick, patched up an old engine, and spudded in, that is, started to drill for oil.

He found his engine in a rusty heap of machinery back of a blacksmith shop. It was worn out and old enough to shave, but Gib rebuilt it, right down to the last gasket.

Now it was puffing bravely, but the ropes on the rig were not moving. Gib looked at the bull wheel, the large spool that held the cables. His gaze followed the rope up to the crown block at the top of the derrick and then down to the drill which was waiting to be dropped into the hole.

"Did you sharpen the drill bit?" he asked.

"Yep," said Toolie, his helper. "She's sharp enough to cut a shadow." He tested the large chisel-shaped drill with his thumb.

"That ought to be sharp enough to cut through the rock when it drops down the well. Are the cables all right?"

"Yep."

"Let's try her once more." Gib engaged the clutch. The big rig trembled, but nothing moved. An unseen force seemed to hold it.

"I ought to do some studyin' an' figgerin' on this," he said. His furrowed brow and close-squinted eyes showed he was in deep thought.

The furrows faded and the squint of his right eye eased. "By

George, there is nothing like a little studyin' an' figgerin'. Now I know what's wrong. The pulleys in the crown block haven't been greased." Shading his eyes from the sun, he peered at the top of the derrick where the rope lines for the drilling tools ran through the pulleys.

"Gee, that's right," Toolie agreed.

"Up you go. Grease 'em good," Gib ordered.

Toolie picked up the grease can, fastened it to his belt, and started to climb to the top of the derrick.

When he reached the top, he waved. Gib waved back.

Toolie waved again. So did Gib.

"That fellow is wavin' like a flag in a windstorm," Gib said as Toolie waved his arm again.

"Eeeeow!" Toolie let out a yell.

"What's the matter? What's wrong?" Gib shouted.

Toolie threw the grease bucket in the air. Spinning like a top, it dropped to the ground and landed with a dull thud.

Meanwhile, Toolie scrambled down the ladder shouting like an Indian on the warpath. When he reached the ground Gib was at his side. "What is it? What happened?" he asked.

"Hornets! Hornets!" Toolie cried out in pain and pointed to his arm.

"Take your shirt off," Gib commanded.

The tool dresser's arm was swollen like a pouter pigeon in a pout.

"Here. Sit on the lazy bench until I come back." Gib helped the man to a small bench at the edge of the derrick floor. "It just so happens I know what to do about hornet stings, on account of I once did some studyin' an' readin' up on that subject."

He turned and started off for the woods at the edge of the clearing in which the drilling rig stood. "I'll be right back straight off," he cried.

He scurried around among the shrubs, stripping leaves from some and peeling a bit of bark from others. When he returned to the rig he opened his tool chest and took out a bottle.

"Venango County crude oil," he said. "It makes fine liniment and such things. It's good for cuts, corns, bruises, dandruff, and rheumatism, and it makes bunions a pleasure."

Gib stooped and ran his hands through the cuttings, the dirt and rock dust that had been taken from the well. He found the special kind he wanted and crushed the leaves, bark, and cuttings together in an empty tin can, adding a carefully measured dollop of Venango County crude oil.

When it was mixed, he touched it softly with his finger and smelled it. "By George," he announced, "it's fine. Don't think I ever made better hornet sting poultice. Here. Let me put some on that arm of yours."

Toolie's arm seemed swollen to the bursting point. Gib daubed it with the poultice. "There. You'll be as good as new in a few minutes," he assured Toolie.

"Look!" Toolie gasped.

The angry red of his arm faded, and the swelling melted like a balloon stuck with a pin. Gib nodded.

"I never saw such a quick cure for a hornet sting," Toolie said with surprise.

Gib smiled. "It's pretty good for almost anything that ails a man," he said modestly.

"And the pain. It's gone! And I sure did have an arm full of pain."

Now Gib was all business again. "Did you get the pulley greased?" he asked.

"Yes. The hornets didn't come until after I was finished."

"Good. Then I'll lower that bit and start drillin'." He engaged the clutch. The engine puffed. The tools began to move. But the rig shuddered to a halt.

Gib moved the clutch again and once more an unseen power proved too strong for the engine. "There is something wrong with the pulleys up on the crown block," Gib declared. "I'll go up and take a look."

"Be careful of hornets," said Toolie.

"This will keep them away," Gib answered as he dabbed some of the poultice on his hands and arms.

He climbed the ladder to the crown block. What he saw

made him gasp. "By George, I never saw a thing like that before," he said.

Gib shouted down. "How's your arm?"

"Fine."

"Come up here. I want to show you something you're never likely to see again. Bring up the hornet sting poultice with you."

Toolie put the small can in his pocket and scrambled up the ladder.

When he reached the top, Gib pointed at the rope running through the pulley. "Look!" he said dramatically.

"Why, that rope looks swollen," said Toolie.

"It *is* swollen," said Gib.

"How could a thing like that happen?"

"It's the hornets," Gib announced solemnly.

"Hornets? But how did that rope get swollen?"

"The hornets stung it."

"But—" Toolie was having trouble finding words.

"A hornet stung your arm and it swelled up, didn't it?" Gib asked.

"Yes—but—"

"All right. Hornets stung the rope and it swelled up too," said Gib simply.

"But that rope is big! It's as big as a watermelon!"

"Well, maybe it is as big as a *small* watermelon," Gib said. "A man should be accurate and never exaggerate. Yep. That rope is swollen up so big it won't run through the pulley."

"It don't seem possible," Toolie said with wonder.

"I know. It didn't seem possible that your arm would swell up so much either. But it did, didn't it?" Gib asked.

"It sure did," Toolie admitted. "But what are we goin' to do?" Then he brightened. "I know. We can cut the swollen place out, and then splice the cable."

"That would take too long. Anyway, I think I know a better way."

"How?"

"We'll put some poultice on the rope, same as on your arm," said Gib quietly.

"Do you think it will work? On a rope?"

"My hornet sting poultice always works," Gib replied with simple dignity. He slathered the poultice on the rope.

As Toolie watched, he became bug-eyed at what he saw. The swollen part of the rope reduced in size until it was the same thickness as the rest of the rope.

"Gee!" Toolie said, and amazement filled his voice.

"Come on. Let's get a string of tools down that hole an' do some diggin'," said Gib. He paused a thoughtful moment. "By George, I never saw my special hornet sting poultice work any better than that," he declared.

2

Gib's Fishing Tool

GIB MORGAN was a modest man. His wit was as bright as a new penny. His mind was as keen as the edge of a razor blade, and he had a smile that was warm enough to send the thermometer up seven degrees. And he was an honest man.

"I always try to tell the truth, the absolute truth," he said. "And sometimes it isn't easy. Sometimes there isn't enough truth to go around."

Oil drillers do not stay in one place. They move on to new fields as they are discovered. Every place Gib went, strange things happened to him, things that never seemed to happen to other drillers.

Every driller needs a tool dresser to help him—to keep the drills sharp, the engine working, and the pulleys greased. Little Toolie was a good worker, but he didn't go to the West Virginia field when it opened up. He stayed home, in Pennsylvania, to help run the pumps.

When oil was discovered in West Virginia, Gib wasted no time getting there. He was hired to dig a well by the Scarcely Able and Hardly Ever Get Oil Company.

Gib thought he had seen steep mountains in Pennsylvania, but in West Virginia, he got a real education in steep hills. "By George," he said, "these hills are so steep you can lean against them when you get tired."

He hired a farmer to be his tool dresser. Gib knew all about oil rigs and was a good teacher. "First off," he said, "you've got to remember a toolie has to work hard. Like a driller. You'll be as busy as three huntin' dogs in a rabbit patch. I'll show you how to sharpen the drills, fire the steam engine, do the greasin', and—you're not afraid to climb to the top of a forty-foot derrick, are you?" he asked.

Frank—that was the farmer's name—looked at Gib Morgan with a smile. "I've been climbin' these hills all my life. They're a lot taller than forty feet."

"Then let's find a location for the rig," said Gib.

"What's a rig?"

"That's what we use to drill for oil with—the derrick, the engine, the boiler, ropes, belts, tools—the works. The derrick has pulleys on top so that drills, pipes, bailers, and tools can be dropped down and pulled up out of the hole we'll dig. The engine supplies the power."

The two men climbed up a narrow, winding trail, pausing at small patches that had been cleared for farming on the steep mountainside wherever there was a level spot big enough for a mule to turn around.

The place Gib picked was a dangerous perch far above a stream that snaked between the steep slopes on each side. Little cabins dotted the hillside on other small plots of level land.

Frank looked over the edge of the tiny corn patch where they were standing. "Maw's got supper ready," he said.

"How do you know that?" Gib asked.

"You can see. Look." He pointed down.

Gib went to his side. Standing at the edge, he too looked down. Below him he saw a little cabin nestling on another narrow ledge below them.

He gasped. "By George! It's true. You can see right down the chimney. The table is all set, and I see pork chops, hominy, potatoes, and turnip greens cooking."

"It sure does look good, don't it?" Frank said.

"Sure does," Gib agreed.

"It works the other way around too. When you're in the house, you can see what's goin' on in the farm patches up above on the hill."

"It's real handy," Gib agreed.

Gib hired a crew. Lumber, heavy equipment, tools, and machines were hauled up the steep, winding trail. The derrick was raised. The engine and the boiler were placed. The lines were strung through the pulleys on the crown block. It was a busy time.

It took a lot of men to build a rig, men who could use tools and who could manage horses and mules. It took muscle and brains. It took words and songs, and shouts and laughter, lumber, iron, steel, and rope. It took all of these things to build an oil rig.

Grandpaw Jake was a tall, lean, old man with a gray grizzled beard and toothless gums. While the rig was going up he usually stood near, chewing on a straw, his long, pointed chin bobbing up and down. When the rig started to work, Grandpaw Jake began chopping weeds in a nearby corn patch.

The drill was moving up and down as the walking beam moved, cutting away at the dirt and rock far below the surface. As the hole went deeper, Gib moved the temper screw to drop the cutting edge of the drill farther and farther into the hole.

"Oops!" Gib frowned.

"What's wrong?" asked Frank.

"We've lost the drill bit. It broke clean off," Gib said. "And when a rope choker like me loses a drill, he's got a real problem."

"The drill bit is away down there in the hole. You can't get it out," said Frank.

"I've got to get it out," Gib replied.

"How? How're you goin' to get it up?"

"I'm goin' to make me a fishin' tool," Gib said. "Something that can latch on to that sixty-pound bit down there and bring her up."

"It don't seem possible to me."

As Gib turned to his task, he explained to Frank. "There are lots of different kinds of fishing tools for different jobs, and more will be invented."

"But it's way down there in the hole. The rope is unfastened and I don't see how you can ever get anything to take hold of that drill bit and bring it up."

"It's got to be some kind of a clamp that works kind of automatic. Some of 'em have names, like two-prong grab, horn socket, cherry picker, boot jacket, center-rope spears, and bulldog spears.

"Each kind suits a different job. They've got to do one thing only. That is, drop down into the hole at the end of the drilling line and grab hold of the drill bit or whatever it is down here. Then they have to hang on so we can pull it up.

"I remember once I made quite a name for myself when I fished out an oak 2 x 4 that no one else could get out. And I didn't use a tool of any kind either."

"How did you do it?" asked Frank.

"I filled the hole up with water, and the piece of wood floated up to the top."

The fire was made bright in the forge. Iron and steel were heated glowing red and bent and shaped with heavy hammers. At last the fishing tool was ready. Gib fastened it to the cable. The heavy device had to work precisely if the job were to be done. It was shaped like a pincers with springs and a trigger.

At the bottom of the well, an attached cord would pull the trigger, the pincers would close on the drill bit, the springs would hold it tightly closed. With a good share of luck and a lot of skill, Gib would be able to raise the bit.

Grandpaw Jake had watched the making of the fishing tool, but when the work was done, the old man had gone back to his corn patch. He was there, resting, leaning on his hoe. Grandpaw Jake was a great rester. He always said he did it because he didn't want to wear out his muscles by working too much. Grandpaw Jake said hard work never killed anybody—but then, neither did resting, and a man ought to play it as safe as possible.

Gib had the new fishing tool in place. He was about to run it down the hole when he heard a sharp crack. It sounded like a stick breaking. Gib looked over to the corn patch. Grandpaw Jake was gone.

It was strange, Gib thought. The old man was there only a moment before. He was standing there, leaning on his hoe handle.

Gib heard a shout. It came from below. He and Frank ran to the small corn patch. They looked over the edge. "By George!" said Gib. "That's some drop down the side of the mountain."

They heard a voice, the weak wavering voice of an old man.

"Look!" cried Frank. "Grandpaw Jake's done fell out of the corn patch!"

Then Gib saw what had happened. The hoe handle had

broken under the strain of Grandpaw Jake's leaning on it, and the old man had tumbled off the edge of the cliff. Fortunately, his suspenders had caught on a stout branch of a haw tree, and his fall had been stopped.

There he was, dangling by his tightly stretched galluses, a hundred feet from the cornfield and three hundred feet from the stony, hard-packed earth below.

Something had to be done! But what? If the suspenders broke, the old man would surely be killed by the fall.

Gib was quick to act. He pushed the new fishing tool off the edge of the ledge. He let out the cable. It dropped down the side of the cliff.

For the first ninety feet it dropped fast. Then Gib slowed it down. Moving the clutch handle carefully, Gib sank the fishing tool slowly toward Grandpaw Jake, who was swinging back and forth in the breeze, like an apple on the tip of a branch.

The fishing tool hovered over the old man. Gib let out some more cable—an inch, half an inch, less, less—a millimeter, half a millimeter, a quarter, less, less. Slowly the heavy fishing tool sank. Gently. Gently.

The time had come. Gib released the trigger he had so skillfully made. The steel springs snapped and the iron prongs closed around the old man, enfolding him in a soft, but strong, grasp of iron.

Gib moved the clutch again. The engine puffed, the bull

wheel lumbered. The old man, waving his arms and legs in space, seemed to fly up to the rig as the pulleys sang. Gib touched the reverse lever and Grandpaw Jake landed at Gib Morgan's side, safe once more at the edge of the ledge.

"Goodness sakes, Grandpaw," said Gib as the old man sat on the ground trying to catch his breath, and wondering how it was that he had been snatched from the arms of death. "You ought to be more careful. It's dangerous to work so close to the edge."

"I wasn't workin'. I was restin'," was the reply. "But I can tell you that was some close shave. Why, my heart is flutterin' like the lid on a boilin' tea kettle."

"You ought to have a fence there," Gib insisted.

"No. I don't need no fence. What I need is a new hoe handle. I knowed the other one was gettin' weak," said Grandpaw sagely.

The new fishing tool worked just as well on the lost drill as it had on Grandpaw Jake. Gib fished it out, and the work in the West Virginia field went on.

3

Gib Morgan Drills a Dry Well

WHEN GIB first saw Texas Toolie, the big fellow was squeezing the juice out of rocks with his fists. He was out of a job, broke, and hungry. There wasn't much nourishment in rock juice, but it was all he had to eat.

Gib felt sorry for the man. "You ought to get a job," he said.

"I can't get one," was the reply.

"Why not?"

"I don't know how to do nothin'. Never had much schoolin'."

"I'll teach you to be a tool dresser," said Gib.

And he did. Before long, the big Texan was known to everyone as Texas Toolie. He was as strong as Gib was smart.

"A man's got to have a trade or something," Gib always said. "It's pretty silly to try to go through life without having a way to earn a living."

The first well Gib dug in Texas was a dry hole. Most oil drillers would have called the well a failure, but not Gib Morgan. He was a man who could turn failure into success.

Gib knew there was oil there, deeper down, but the company brass hats told him to stop drilling. They said if he dug any deeper he would bring in a well in China.

The company brass hats told him to plug up the hole. It was quite a hole and Gib was proud of it from a technical point of view. He didn't want it to go to waste.

Just about that time Gib met a cattleman named Tex. His spread was so big he could ride all day and not get out of the calf pasture.

"I need a new calf pasture," Tex told Gib. "But my cow-punchers don't want to dig postholes. They say if they can't do it on horseback they don't want to do it. And you certainly can't dig a posthole from the top of a horse."

Gib nodded his understanding. Everyone had problems, it seemed.

Tex shook his head sadly. "But why am I botherin' you with my troubles? You've got enough trouble with your dry hole."

"I'm doin' some studyin' an' figgerin' on it," said Gib.

The two men sat silently for a few moments, their rocking chairs squeaking as they rocked back and forth on Tex's porch.

"By George, I think maybe I've got it," Gib said quietly.

"Got what?" Tex asked.

"I could pull up my dry hole and cut it into short lengths and

CO. SCHOOLS
C850730

you could use them for postholes!'"

"Gib, you are a genius! That's as slick a trick as I ever heard. Yes sir, as slick as greased lard."

The idea worked fine. Gib had enough dry hole for all the postholes Tex needed. Besides that, there was enough left over to make three wells for water which Tex was very glad to have.

4

Gib's Big Rig

It is not likely that anyone will ever sink a well deeper than Gib Morgan did with his big rig.

It was in West Texas, and it was Gib who brought in the first well out there. Of course, out there, everything is bigger than anywhere else. It stands to reason that is where Gib dug his deep well.

"I know there is oil there, but I've got to dig a real deep ditch to reach it," Gib said.

"How deep?" Big Texas Toolie asked.

"The deepest hole ever dug," Gib replied.

Gib ordered special tools and began to build the derrick. Each of the four sides of the rig was as long as he could throw a baseball with the wind at his back. It was so high that Gib had it hinged in the middle so that flying geese and ducks could go past. It was right in the middle of a flyway. In the spring and fall, when the birds were on their way north or south, he would bend the top over on its hinges. Not a single bird was killed in all the time the big rig was in operation.

Gib's derrick was so tall it took a grease monkey fourteen days to climb to the top to grease the crown pulleys, and the pulleys were so big they had to be greased every day.

He figured it would take thirty men to work as grease monkeys and he put Big Texas Toolie in charge of them.

He built bunk houses on the derrick a day's climb from each other. The brass hats took a great deal of interest in the big rig, so that Gib wouldn't have all the glory. They ordered hot and cold· running water put in the bunk houses. They took that part of the job away from Gib, and they didn't do it right. It turned out that the water was hot in the summer and cold in the winter.

Gib tried to get the bosses to change things around and have hot and cold water at the same time. He reported the facts to the home office, but as everyone knows, brass hats are not easy to argue with. Finally he had to step in and make things right.

It worked out that fourteen grease monkeys were climbing up the derrick all the time. Fourteen more grease monkeys were coming down all the time. There would be one at the top each day greasing the pulleys, and one at the bottom, getting ready to start to climb to the top.

As soon as the derrick was built, the special tools Gib had ordered began to arrive at the location.

"What's them?" Big Texas Toolie asked.

"Tools. The one on that first special flat car is the drilling tool I am going to spud in with," Gib explained.

"But that drill stem must be eight, maybe nine, feet wide."

"Eight feet, exactly," said Gib.

They got the string of tools together and spudded in.

Some men never learn the art of drilling. Some men learn to do it quite well. But a top driller such as Gib Morgan is born with his skill. Such men know by a strange sense what condition the drilling tools are in when they are working deep in the earth. They know where gumbo, sand, clay, stone, or shale will begin and end.

"Hold it!" Gib said suddenly. "The sand is goin' to cave in if we don't put a casing in to hold it back."

The casing was made of thousand-gallon oil drums riveted together. When the casing was made it was dropped down into the hole where it would hold the sand back. Then Gib put on a seven-foot drill and dug another stretch of hole before he had to case it off and use a still smaller drill.

Down and down the drills went, each one smaller than the one used before. The casings followed, each smaller than the other, to fit each new drill hole and keep the hole tight, so that water and sand could not enter.

"We're down to a two-foot drill," announced Gib.

Soon he began to use standard-size tools. The work went on and it was not long until he had to make some special small tools.

"What are you goin' to do if you don't strike oil before you get down to a casing so small you can't get tools through it?" asked Big Texas Toolie.

Gib's eyes steeled. "That's not goin' to happen," he said grimly.

"That last casing was pretty small. It was only an inch wide. It looked pretty silly fastened onto a two-inch cable."

"I studied and I figgered for this job. There is oil down there, and I am going to reach it!" said Gib.

They dropped down a casing that was only half an inch wide.

"Maybe you figgered it too fine," said Texas Toolie.

"Fine, maybe, but not too fine!" Gib declared stubbornly.

"What are you goin' to do?" Toolie asked. "That last casing is so small, there ain't no smaller bit that can be made that will go in it."

"I won't be stumped by that!"

"What are you goin' to do?"

Gib's eyes lighted up. "I studied and figgered on this, and I can't be wrong. Just get me a needle and thread," he said suddenly.

"But Gib—you can't—"

"It's my last chance. I know I've got to strike oil here! I figgered it!"

Big Texas Toolie brought a needle and thread. Gib strung them on the drilling line.

He pulled the lever. The big wheels clanked and turned.

Pulleys rumbled as the needle and thread dropped down the big hole into the massive void, down to the bottom of the well it had taken so long to dig.

The grease monkeys and the roustabouts knew of the hope and pride and faith that were crowded at the tip of the tiny point as the dirty cable rumbled down into the black depths.

The walking beam moved. The steam engine hissed and groaned like a giant at labor. And far below, a slender tip of steel struck against the bottom of the hole. Again, and again, and again, and again.

"There's not much power down there, but every little bit helps," said Gib hopefully.

There was a faint hissing sound. Gib's ears seemed to stretch out to catch the noise. There was a small, distant rumble. Gib's eyes sparkled with a wonderful light, a light bright enough to read by on a dark night.

A long, delicate, slender spout of dark oil rose in a straight line out of the depths of the black hole.

The black stream rose higher and splattered against the crown block of the world's tallest derrick. The oil fell back on the floor and on the happy driller whose grin spread from ear to ear. It was a grin so wide it hurt.

"It's a gusher!" cried Big Texas Toolie.

"It sure is," Gib agreed. "A slender gusher. Only as thick as a needle, but a gusher!"

The small hissing sound became a large roar. The thin stream

of oil became a thick stream as the great pressures in the earth below blew the smallest casings out of the hole.

Grease monkeys and roustabouts joined the tool maker and Gib Morgan in cheers and whoops of joy.

"Texas Toolie," said Gib, as he wiped the fresh drops of petroleum from his face with a greasy hand, "we have struck oil! But I sure did figger it down to a fine point!"

5

Gib, the Innkeeper

MEN WHO WORK in oil fields are always on the move, for oil, like gold, is where you find it. The search for black gold never stops.

When a new field is brought in, swarms of men in every branch of the oil business are drawn to it. Each man, in his own way, hopes for some of the riches that will flow from the dark fluid.

The first needs of the men at new fields are for food and places to live. Tents and field kitchens soon are replaced by boardinghouses and hotels.

Once, Gib started a new business because he knew how to make fine pancakes. He was living in a tent then, and he made some extra pancakes for his neighbors. More and more men came around looking neighborly, so he offered them some pancakes too. So many men wanted his pancakes that he decided to open a restaurant. Soon there were so many customers he stirred up the batter in concrete mixers.

The mixers and the engines that ran them were up on top of a hill. The batter was carried to the kitchen by a pipeline. He used the bottoms of 43,000-barrel oil tanks for griddles and heated them with gas piped from a gas well he had sunk. Seven men with sides of bacon strapped to their feet skated on the griddles to grease them.

Another crew squirted batter from hoses, and another turned the pancakes and tossed them to waiters who sped on roller skates to the hungry customers.

Melted butter, syrup, honey, coffee, milk, and tea were piped down the center of the table so that the customers could get anything they wanted by turning a tap.

Gib's griddlecakes were so good and he had so many customers that he could have stayed in the business and have made a lot of money. But he was an oil man. He only got into the restaurant business to help the hungry men who had come to the new field. When another field was discovered a few hundred miles away in West Texas, he sold out and went out there.

Thousands of men were crowding into the new area. They had no good place to stay. Gib wanted to help them too, so he decided to build a hotel. He had some new ideas he wanted to try out.

Gib noticed that out there in the Southwest, guests always asked for a south or an east room. He wanted his guests to be happy and have the kind of rooms they asked for, so he decided to build a hotel without any north or west rooms. It took some studying and figuring, but he did it.

His hotel had forty stories and ten high-speed elevators. There were narrow-gauge trains on each floor to speed the guests to their rooms.

In each room he put a number of faucets—for cold water, hot water, ice water, fruit juice, coffee, tea, cocoa, and milk.

He solved the problem of putting everyone in a south or an east room by building the hotel on a giant turntable.

First, he would fill all of the south rooms. Then, he would assign guests to the east rooms. When those in the south rooms were asleep, he would start the turntable and the east rooms would become south rooms and north rooms would become east rooms.

Then, when the guests in the east rooms, which had become the south rooms, went to sleep, he would start the turntable again and give the hotel another quarter turn, and the rooms which had been the east rooms (but which had become the south rooms) would become the west rooms, while the rooms which had been the west rooms and which had become the north rooms, became the east rooms.

This went on until all the rooms were filled and the hotel had turned completely around and the south rooms were back where they had started and so were all of the other rooms.

Naturally, the guests who had gone to bed first awakened first and there they were in their south rooms. When they were up and checked out, Gib would start the turntable again so that the north rooms became the east rooms, and the east rooms became the south rooms, while the west rooms would become the north rooms, and at the next quarter turn, when it was time to get up, those guests would be in the east rooms.

At first Gib thought some people might object to this because, in a way, they weren't really always in south or east rooms. Still, in another way, they were, for they were given the kinds of rooms they asked for, went to sleep in them, and woke up in them.

Most of the guests didn't find out what had happened. Why should they? They went to sleep in south or east rooms. It really didn't make much difference to them where they had been during the night when they were asleep.

The few guests who discovered what had happened didn't mind. In fact, they were pleased with it all. The fast elevators were thrilling and the narrow-gauge railway trip to the rooms was interesting. The spigot service was excellent, and the turntable trip at night was exciting to those who might be awake.

Some insomniacs and those who were light sleepers, and who had spent many lonely hours trying to find agreeable ways to pass sleepless nights, came back over and over again just for the ride.

6

Gib Morgan at Pikes Peak

WHATEVER Gib's troubles were in the mountains of West Virginia, they didn't compare to the time he went to Colorado to drill a well.

Big Texas Toolie was with him. The geologists had picked a location and had marked it with a cross on a map. The two men looked at each other with amazement. Then they looked at their map again to make sure there had been no mistake.

"It can't be true," said Big Texas Toolie.

"But it is," Gib replied.

"The rockhound who picked such a spot for an oil well location has got a rock head," Toolie said.

"True. But the geologist put the cross here on the map. And it's smack dab on the top of Pikes Peak."

"Must of been some rock puppy who did that."

"All right. Maybe it was a young geologist, but there is the mark, and that is where we'll have to spud in, even though I don't think we'll strike oil there," Gib said.

He looked at the vast area that stretched away to the horizon. "You can see so far up here that your eyes get tired from lookin' all that distance," he added.

"But you can never put a rig up and dig a hole on the top of Pikes Peak. There ain't a level spot that's big enough," Big Texas Toolie insisted.

"I'm a rope choker, a driller. I don't have to be kicked from behind in order to go ahead. When I've got a job to do, I do it. I set a lot of store in the fact that I never yet saw a location I couldn't drill on," Gib said with quiet dignity.

"Where you goin' to put the engine and the boiler?"

"We're goin' to put them on the closest level place that is near wood for the fire for the steam engine," said Gib.

"Where will that be?"

"Right here." Gib's heavy finger pointed to a spot on the map. "It's twenty-three miles from the derrick as I calculate it."

"Twenty-three miles! You can't have a belt twenty-three miles long!"

"The belt will be forty-six miles long because it has to go from the engine to the derrick, and back. As I figger it, that will make it the longest belt in the world. And I figger too, that a belt like that will stretch a good deal."

They hauled the lumber for the derrick on the backs of sure-footed Rocky Mountain mules. It was quickly built. The boiler and engine were located near Colorado Springs.

The forty-six-mile-long belt from the engine to the derrick was soon in place. Gib was right. It did stretch. Every few days he would take the slack out of it. He accumulated a supply of extra leather that was used to half-sole and heel the boots of the whole crew all the time the job was going on and for three-and-a-half years afterward.

A driller and a toolie have to go back and forth between the power plant and the derrick quite often. Gib used burros and mountain mules. Rocky Mountain canaries, they were called, because they brayed, or sang so much.

They rode the sure-footed animals back and forth over the steep trail. Of course, Big Texas Toolie was too big for one mule to carry. He had to ride two mules. He was too big to even try to ride burros, so no one knows how many of those he would have required.

"I heard of a fellow named Sergeant O'Keefe who lived in these parts. He used to operate the weather station on top of Pikes Peak. I wish we had the kind of mule he had," Gib said.

"What kind did he have?" Toolie asked.

"Her name was Balaam. She was an extraordinary mule," Gib replied.

"How's that?"

"Why Balaam could walk up and down the steepest places, even cliffs. She sort of hung on, like a fly."

"I sure wouldn't want to be ridin' her then," said Toolie.

"Then, Balaam had ears that were so big and she could move 'em so fast that she could fly. But I guess there's not any more mules like her. I've got to do some studyin' an' figgerin' about a better way to go back and forth between the power plant and the derrick," Gib declared.

After some studying and figuring, Gib said, "I found it. I found a better way for us to travel between the engine and the tower."

"How?" Toolie asked.

"Why, we will just throw our saddles over the belt. The belt is runnin' all the time. We will ride the belt back and forth!"

"By golly, that's a fine idea!" Toolie shouted.

"Come on," the driller cried. "Let's ride!"

He tossed his saddle over the belt and pulled the cinches tight. Toolie did the same.

"Here we go!" Gib sang out as he swung into the saddle. "We'll go lopin' along somewhere between the sky and earth. There's no cowpuncher who ever lived who had such a high-flyin', moon-climbin' ride as we've got right here!"

The two men went riding off into space toward the derrick, twenty-three miles away.

"Yippee! Git along little dogie!" Gib shouted.

"Yippee!" Toolie cried, and the echoes bounced back and forth among the foothills and the canyons of Pikes Peak.

7

The Grand Jibbonancy of the Itsy Bitsy Island

THE Noble, Grand, Worshipful, Master, Chancellor, Commander, Exalted Ruler, and Jibbonancy of the Itsy Bitsy Island asked Gib to come and sink a well on his island. Big Texas Toolie went with him.

Gib didn't think there was oil to be found at the location, and said so.

"Your Jibbonancy," he said, "I don't think you will find oil here. You may find a lot of other things, but not oil. You ought to get some rockhounds and pebble puppies, and get their advice."

But his Jibbonancy insisted, and so Gib spudded in exactly as he was directed.

At 2,000 feet he struck some pink and white sand. Soon there was a flow of green liquid.

He smelled it. "Smells like peppermint," he said.

He tasted it. "Tastes like peppermint," he said.

He looked at it. "Looks like peppermint," he said.

He drew his breath sharply, almost unable to believe his senses. He slapped his fist in his hand. "By George, it *is* peppermint!" he declared.

It was a small, steady flow and Gib wanted to stop drilling because he had a good-paying well. "We better stop drilling, Your Jibbonancy," he said. "With this flow, you can have the Peppermint Capital of the World."

"I will not hear of it," His Jibbonancy replied. "It is oil I want. Good old-fashioned petroleum oil. Dig, and I will have the Oil Capital of the World."

Much against his better judgment, Gib sank casing and cased off the flow of essence of peppermint and resumed drilling.

Soon the sand changed color. It was bright red. He rolled it between his fingers. He eyed it curiously. He smelled it. He could scarcely believe what his senses told him.

"Unless I am wrong, which in all honesty I've got to admit is not often the case," he announced, "we will have a good flow of hair tonic before nightfall."

When the hair tonic began to flow, he hurried toward the grass and palm leaf mansion of His Jibbonancy.

"Your Jibbonancy!" he exclaimed. "We have struck a good flow of hair tonic!"

"Hair tonic will not do. It is oil I must have," the ruler announced curtly.

"But, Your Jibbonancy! We could tap in the essence of peppermint and have peppermint-scented hair tonic. You could make a fortune."

"I don't want a fortune. I have a fortune. No. No hair tonic. No essence of peppermint. Petroleum!"

"If we struck a small vein of oil, we could have scented hair tonic and hair oil."

"No hair oil either. Petroleum!"

Gib cased off the hair tonic and began to drill again.

About 600 feet below the hair tonic, he got a strong flow of a white liquid. Gib touched the stuff with his tongue. His face blossomed into a grin. "It's cream. That's what it is. It's cream!"

Gib was surprised when His Jibbonancy ordered the drilling stopped. "Cream! With cream we can make ice cream," the Exalted Ruler said as he spread his tongue over his lips and his hands over his ample belly, happy with the thought of the cold, sweet treat to come.

"Get the machinery! Order the necessary machinery. We will make an ice cream factory," he declared.

"But, Your Jibbonancy—"

"Yes. What?"

"I don't recommend it."

The monarch became stern. "First, you wanted to stop with peppermint. I did not want to. Then you wanted to stop at hair tonic. Then you spoke of hair oil and tonic, some such thing.

That did not please me." He paused to search his memory.

"But now, I want to stop at the cream, and you raise objections." He scowled. "Mr. Morgan, I am afraid you do not realize that I am the Noble, Exalted Ruler, and Jibbonancy of the Itsy Bitsy Island. What I say is the law of this land! And I say we will stop at this lovely flow of sweet cream and I will build an ice cream factory!" Once again he smacked his lips and patted his belly.

"But, Your Jibbonancy, I wish to point out—"

"Enough! I, the Supreme Jibbonancy, have spoken!" He made a grand and final gesture.

After a pause he continued in a more gentle tone. "I must remind you, Mr. Morgan, that you are an oil driller. A master oil driller, it is true, perhaps *the* master oil driller. As you say, a rope choker. You are, in a way, a king too. The king of your profession. I do not want you to think I do not appreciate your great talents and your skill in bringing in this wonderful oil well. Ahem, I mean, this wonderful cream well."

"All right, if that's what you say, we will pull our tools and set the Christmas tree to top it off. But I don't recommend it, and I think you ought to let me tell you why." Gib was very serious.

His Jibbonancy smiled and shook his head.

"That Jibbonancy ought to learn to listen and to take advice," Gib said to Big Texas Toolie as they left the palace.

Gib and Toolie set the Christmas tree, the elaborate arrangement of valves that would control the flow of the cream.

When the machinery arrived Gib built the ice cream factory. He didn't want to do it, but he was under contract, so he followed orders. He knew what the awful result would be. He wished His Jibbonancy would listen to what he had to say.

The factory was finished. His Jibbonancy came to the plant to watch the first flow of cream come from the well. He was a proud and happy man when he turned the valve and saw the creamy liquid flow into the vats of the ice cream factory.

He made a speech then, and he made another speech when he was handed the first dish of ice cream. He was a dramatic figure in his scarlet and gold uniform. He glowed as he lifted the first spoonful to his mouth. He smiled as his lips closed on it.

Then his back stiffened, his cheeks puffed out. His eyebrows lifted to the place where his hairline once had been.

"What is this?" he thundered in a roar that made his medals jangle.

Gib stepped forward. One look, one smell, let him know his worst fears had come true. One taste proved it. It was just what he had expected. The cream had turned sour.

His Jibbonancy stamped and stormed and roared, but he could not blame Gib. The master rope choker had wanted to tell him the cream would sour, had tried to tell him.

When His Jibbonancy regained his poise, he turned to Gib. "Dig deeper!" he commanded.

"Now, see here, Your Jibbonancy, we have had a lot of luck on this well. I think it has been good luck. You think it has been bad luck, but you've got to admit it has been strange luck, and that is better than no luck at all. Now, sometimes a man just plain runs out of luck, and I don't think it is a good idea to dig any more." Gib was warming to his subject, but His Jibbonancy interrupted.

"Mr. Morgan, I have spoken!" he declared.

Gib went on. "If we stop now, you can have all the sour cream and berries a country could wish for. And then there are sour cream biscuits. And sour cream—"

"Dig!" His Jibbonancy thundered.

"You are lucky it's not worse. Why—"

"Luck waits for courage! Dig!"

"You're runnin' out of luck," Gib warned.

"Dig!"

"All right, if you say so, but I don't recommend it," Gib declared defiantly.

Gib dropped the string of drilling tools into the hole. He dug twenty feet and it was all over. He struck salt water.

"Just what I figgered would happen," he said to Big Texas Toolie. "We have gone through the bottom of the Island of Itsy Bitsy, and the ocean down below has flooded up and filled the hole."

As the salt water came up, the island sank. There was no way to case off the salt water.

Gradually all of the island disappeared. That is the reason the island of Itsy Bitsy cannot be found on any modern maps. As Gib always said, it never would have happened that way if His Jibbonancy had followed his advice.

8

Gib Goes to South America

SOME OF Gib's most interesting adventures happened the time he went wildcatting in South America.

Before he left the United States, the brass hats told him not to go down more than 10,000 feet. So, naturally, he ordered only 10,000 feet of rope to take along with him. He didn't believe in spending money unless it was absolutely necessary. As a businessman he was as hardheaded as a woodpecker.

It was a good location, but the mosquitoes were terrible. The men were miserable. There were so many mosquitoes that they blocked out the moon.

Gib picked up his twenty-four-barrel shotgun and blasted away. He made a hole in the mosquitoes big enough to let in some moonlight. "Quick! We've got to build a shelter," he cried.

He held the big insects off with his shotgun while he directed Big Texas Toolie and the roustabouts in the building of a shelter. It was little more than a stake wall with a cover on it, but it protected them from the fierce insects. The spaces between the stakes were only about four inches wide, and the big mosquitoes couldn't get through the cracks.

Gib sat up all night with his good old shotgun ready, but there was no more trouble. The mosquitoes went away. Gib wondered why. The next morning he found out.

The mosquitoes had carried away the team of horses the crew had been using. They took them down to the river and ate them. When Gib went down there the next day he found a pile of bones. Farther down the stream he saw the mosquitoes. Some of them were sitting on a log picking their teeth with horseshoe nails. The rest of the mosquitoes were playing horseshoes.

Gib built some better shelters and kept his shotgun handy. Not many mosquitoes came to the camp after that, but Gib knew they would remain a problem and wanted to be ready for them if they did come back.

"We've got to do something about these mosquitoes," he said.

"Yes, but what?" asked Big Texas Toolie.

"I'll show you. I have been doin' some studyin' an' figgerin' on it. By the looks of things, I think I'll find what I'm lookin' for right over there." He pointed to an outcropping of rocks.

He put up a small derrick. Then he spudded in, and at three hundred feet, struck a vein of quinine.

"I never saw a quinine well before. Never even heard of one," said Big Texas Toolie, unable to conceal his surprise.

"You've got to pick your location exactly right. Not many drillers can do it," Gib said modestly. "And I figger I can strike oil of citronella if I spud in over there beyond that knoll about 500 feet to the northeast of here."

"What do you want that for?" asked Toolie.

"Why, quinine is the remedy for malaria, which comes from mosquitoes. And oil of citronella is supposed to keep mosquitoes away," Gib answered.

"There are a lot of real tough mosquitoes in these parts," he went on. "So we have to try to keep them away, and we have to have a cure for malaria."

Toolie nodded in agreement.

"I always like to be prepared," said Gib.

At 400 feet he brought in the oil of citronella well. They didn't have much trouble with the insects after that.

The mosquitoes that were tough enough to stand the smell of the oil of citronella were tough enough to bite an oil man. But they found the quinine distasteful. Besides, their stingers were always sore because they had to push so hard to get through the tough hides of the oil men.

9

Jungle Cable

WITH THE mosquito problem over, the derrick in South America was soon set up and the drilling for oil started.

One day Gib looked curiously at the bull wheel. There was no more rope wound around it. "Something is wrong," he said. "We are out of cable and we are only down 5,000 feet. I ordered 10,000 feet of rope. I guess some pencil-pushing vice president in the front office made a mistake."

"What are you goin' to do?" asked Texas Toolie.

"I'll just cut the rope in two," said Gib quietly.

"But—"

"Nothing to it. If you have a line 5,000 feet long and you cut it in two, you'll have two lines, won't you?"

"Yes, but—"

"And two times 5,000 is 10,000, isn't it?"

"Yes, but—"

"And 10,000 feet is what we need, isn't it?"

"Well—"

"All right, then. Let's get busy and cut the line. We've got to make sure we cut it exactly in half. If we make a mistake, we won't have enough line. If we cut a thousand feet off, we'll have only 6,000 feet because 5,000 plus 1,000 is only 6,000. While we're at it, we'll cut the sand line, too, because we have only 5,000 feet of that. If we don't, we won't be able to use the sand line to drop the bailer down into the hole. The bailer has to fill up with sand and mud down at the bottom, so we can lift the debris out. If we don't keep the hole cleaned out, we can't keep on diggin'. Yes, sir, that sand line and the bailer are almost as important as the drill bit, the cutting tool."

One day Gib studied the sand brought up in the bailer as it spilled out the material the drill had cut loose. "I'm worried," he said.

"Why?" asked Texas Toolie.

"We are down to oil sand."

"What's there to worry about then?"

"We almost have a paying hole and we are out of line again. We are down to 10,000 feet," Gib said grimly. He looked as unhappy as a woodpecker with a sore beak.

"The front office told me to go only 10,000 feet. But I know we will strike oil if we could go deeper." Gib paused to ponder.

"We've got to have more cable, but I don't want to waste time writin' to the brass hats and orderin' more."

"You can't fight the front office," said Toolie sourly.

"I'm goin' to do some studyin' an' figgerin' on this," said Gib.

He went for a walk in the jungle. He was pondering as he walked slowly. Then he came upon a big snake. Gib looked at it in amazement. As his eyes ran along the length of the reptile he was struck, not only by its length, but also by its sinuous beauty. "By George, that snake must be twenty blocks long. He's even too long to lie about."

The snake had just swallowed a big dinner and he was sound asleep. "I've got an idea," said Gib suddenly.

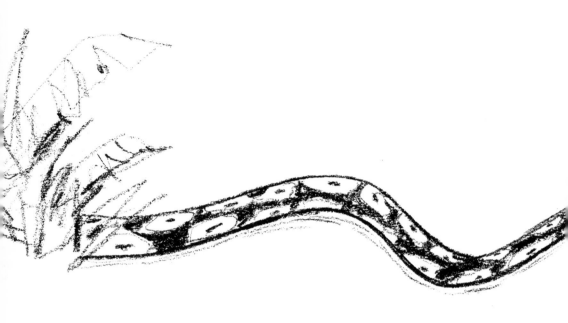

He went back to the rig and called together some of the roustabouts and took them back to the jungle. The snake was still asleep. "Pick him up and carry him to the location," he said.

When the men reached the rig, Gib said, "Bring him here and tie his neck to the spoke of the bull wheel."

The long reptile was wound around the bull wheel and his tail was tied to the end of the drilling rope. "There. Now I've got twenty blocks more line than I had," Gib said. In no time at all he was drilling again.

"By George, that snake makes a good drilling cable," said

Gib. "It's lots better than a new hemp cable. He's got some give
to him. Makes the tools easier to handle."

"Yep. Looks O.K.," Big Texas Toolie agreed.

"I wonder how he's going to take it when he digests his
dinner and wakes up," Gib said. "I've heard that a boa constrictor sleeps a long time after a big dinner. Maybe he'll give
us a little warning, and we can get another big dinner in him
and he'll go to sleep again. If we don't he may get as excited as
a sackful of wildcats."

"You got a problem all right," Toolie said.

"That's real interesting. We've got a critter here that works while he's asleep. He's doin' a fine job and he doesn't even know it. Maybe he'll stay asleep long enough for us to strike oil."

But that was not to be. When the big snake woke up, there was no warning and no chance to give him another meal. The reptile gave his head a twist, and in an instant he had unknotted his neck. He gave his tail a shake, but the knot there didn't untie.

"Look out!" cried Gib.

"Hold him!" shouted Big Texas Toolie.

But it was no use. A man might just as well have tried to hold the wind.

"He's goin' to get away!" Gib was in despair.

The boa constrictor twitched a few twitches. Then he squirmed a few squirms, wiggled a few wiggles, shook a few shakes, and away he went, pulling the cable and the whole string of drilling tools, which were tied to his tail, after him.

"What are we goin' to do now?" wailed Big Texas Toolie.

"I'm goin' to do some studyin' an' figgerin' on it, that's what I'm goin' to do," said Gib firmly. "You know, some folks stand around twiddlin' their thumbs. Others twiddle their tongues. But I'm not goin' to do either. I'm goin' to work and get something done!"

In a few moments his mind was made up. "I didn't do right by that poor boa constrictor," he said. "I liked that snake, not only because he was good looking and strong, and not only because he made a fine drilling line, but because he was a nice snake."

"Yep. I kind of liked him too," said Toolie.

"And I put him to work without his knowledge and consent. I feel real bad about that. I'm as unhappy about that as if I was a hoptoad sittin' in the middle of an acre of thumbtacks. I've got to do right by that snake."

"How can a man do right by a snake?"

"A man can do right by anything, including a snake," Gib replied. "And I'll show you how. I'll apologize. I'm going to treat him kindly and be his friend."

"Be a friend to a snake?" asked Toolie doubtfully.

"Yes, sir. Anybody, anything, will respond to friendship. First off, I want some natives who know the jungle. I want them to track him down. I'd do it myself, because I'm quite a tracker, if I do say so myself, but I'm goin' to be busy. When they find him, I want him brought back here. I'll be ready then to do the right thing by that snake, I hope."

10

Strickie

GIB SET UP a new rig 250 feet south of the quinine well.

"What are you drillin' for now?" Texas Toolie asked.

"It's a long chance I'm takin'," Gib replied. "I want to correct the wrong I did to that poor critter."

A long file of natives came over the hill. "They got him! They are carryin' the snake," Gib cried. He and Texas Toolie ran toward them.

"We got 'um snake. Him very sickee. Him heap thin snake. Him sickee," the chief explained.

And he was thin indeed. Gib looked at the snake, and he was filled with sorrow. "Sickee? Oh, you mean he's sick."

"Yes. That's what I say. Sickee," the chief said.

"Chief, you just gave me an idea. I've been wondering what I might call that boa constrictor. First off, I thought of Bo."

"Bo. From boa. That would be a good name," said Toolie.

"Then I thought of calling him Con, or Connie. From con-strictor, of course."

"That would have been a good name too. Either of them."

"But, chief, when you said he was sickee, I got the best idea of all. I'm going to call him Strickie. That's from constrictor. See?"

"Yes. Me see."

"Say, that's a wonderful name," said Toolie.

"Me think so too," said the chief.

"Yes, sir," said Gib as he fondly patted the ailing reptile on the head. "Strickie. But right now, he's a sickee Strickie."

Gib was as sad as a cowboy without a horse. The eyes of the snake and the man met, and a deep, mutual affection was born. Strickie had every right to be offended because of the rough treatment he had received. But when the snake saw Gib's sorrow-filled face, regret and affection met and mixed. Companionship was born.

Gib's eyes sped over every kink and curve in the long, thin body. The cable was still tied to Strickie's tail.

"Look at our drilling tools. Why, they are small! That drill stem's no bigger than a crowbar."

He knew right away what had happened. "Why, I declare. Strickie has been pullin' that string of tools around after him for so long and so far and so fast, he has worn them down thin."

"It don't seem possible," said Toolie.

"But it is," Gib said soberly. "And it stands to reason it would

be that way. The poor snake has worn himself thin by wigglin'
so many miles through the jungle. It stands to reason that the
tools he was pullin' along after him would be worn down thin
too."

His affection and sympathy for Strickie swelled. Strickie
responded with yet warmer trust shining in the depths of his
beautiful eyes.

"Yes, sir," Gib said quietly, humble before the enduring
qualities of the jungle boa constrictor. It was a solemn moment
as snake eyes and man eyes locked in mutual respect.

The man spoke soberly. "I found you sleeping peacefully as
you were digestin' your dinner, and I dragged you off and tied
knots in your neck and tail. I put you to work without so much
as if you please. I don't know why I did it. Thoughtless, I
guess, because I always make a point to be kind to dumb critters.
And now I'm goin' to win your friendship with kindness. Give
me the quinine, Toolie."

"You goin' to give him quinine?"

"Certainly. In his weakened condition he might catch
malaria. I can't take any chances."

Tenderly, he dosed the snake with quinine. Strickie
swallowed it and made a wry face. "Now, take a dose of
this Venango County crude oil tonic I always carry with me."

Strickie opened his mouth and received the tonic. He made
another face.

"Never you mind, Strickie. It's good for you when you are

ailin' the way you are," Gib said tenderly. Strickie smiled a wan smile and wagged his tail feebly.

Gib massaged Strickie's tail and neck where the knots had been. "You've got to have a little nourishment," he said.

"What are you goin' to give him?" asked Toolie.

"Buttermilk."

"Buttermilk?"

"That's right. Buttermilk."

"Where you goin' to get the buttermilk 'way out here in the jungle?"

"I've already got it." Gib smiled happily. "I spudded in just south of the quinine vein. It was like I figured. It's not a very big flow, maybe runnin' only about twelve to fifteen barrels a day. But it ought to be enough for Strickie and it will help him get back on his feet again—I mean, maybe it will help him get back on his belly—get his health back, you know."

"You certainly think of everything, Gib. And you can do just about everything too," said Big Texas Toolie with admiration.

"I guess you're right about that. But I'm a modest man. So, of course, I can't boast about it or anything like that."

Strickie lapped his buttermilk eagerly. He took only about a quarter of a barrel at first, but as time went on his appetite improved and he began to put on a little flesh. His fine, green color freshened, and soon he was a healthy, happy snake.

Gib was delighted one day when Strickie finished his buttermilk, slipped his forked tongue over his lips to rescue every last drop, and wiggled to the silent rig. His beautiful snake eyes were bright enough to make a rooster crow.

"Look at Strickie," Gib said. It was not necessary to speak because everyone was watching.

Strickie knotted his neck around a spoke in the bull wheel, coiled himself around the drum, and wiggled his tail invitingly.

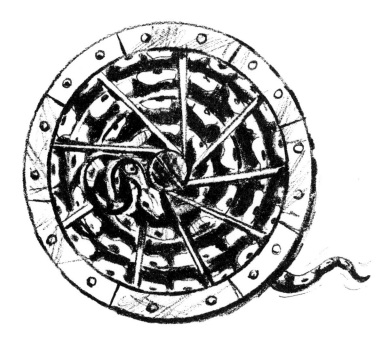

"By George, he wants to go to work," said Gib. He turned to Toolie. "Get up a head of steam," he commanded.

In a short time the steam was up. Strickie's tail was tied to the drilling line. A new string of tools was rigged and they were in operation once more.

Gib declared that Strickie made the best drilling line he had ever used. He had just the right amount of give to make the tools work their best. And then, too, his keen snake intelligence helped a great deal. He could take the kinks out of himself and even out of the rope when it was necessary.

Each night after supper, Strickie coiled himself up in front of the master rope choker's bunk house. Neither man nor beast could come near unless Gib told Strickie it was all right. Gib always said Strickie was the most valuable piece of equipment he ever had.

11

A New Bailing Line

"WE'VE GOT to bail out the cuttings," said Gib. "Get the bailer ready."

The bailer was a long tube the size of the smallest casing in the hole. Fastened to the sand line, it would be dropped down the hole. At the bottom of the well, water would be added to make a slush of the dirt or rock cuttings. A valve on the end of the bailer would open and the slush would enter. Then the valve would close as the bailer was drawn up to the surface and dumped on the cuttings pile. The hole thus emptied would once again permit the drill to drop to the bottom and there cut and chip until it was necessary to take the cuttings out again.

"By George, I'm stuck once more," Gib said suddenly.

"What's wrong now?" asked Texas Toolie as he worked on the bailer to get it ready to drop to the bottom.

"I've only got 10,000 feet of sand line for the bailer. We are down more than 10,000 feet, but we made the drill rope longer by adding Strickie to it. I guess I've got to use Strickie for this too. That will make the sand line as long as the drill line. I'll tie his neck to the rope and his tail to the bailer."

Strickie was taken off the bull wheel and Gib began to place the snake so that his neck could be tied to the sand line. But when the reptile was in the right position, he turned the other way around.

"Strickie is acting mighty peculiar," Gib said. "It's not like him to be stubborn. I've got to do some studyin' an' figgerin' on this. Let's see. He seems to want to work on the sand line all right. But he doesn't want to have his neck tied to it."

He tried once more to tie Strickie's neck to the rope. But again Strickie struggled away and put his tail toward the rope.

Gib snapped his fingers and his thoughtful, furrowed brow evened out. "I know," he declared. "Now all on earth that snake wants is to have his tail tied to the rope so that his neck can be tied to the bailer. He wants to go down into the hole headfirst instead of tailfirst. He wants to see what's going on down there most likely. No wonder he's such a smart snake. He's got a lot of curiosity. He investigates. He thinks."

Gib shrugged. "Well, it doesn't make the least bit of difference to me. I thought he might not like to get the slush in his face."

In a few minutes Strickie's tail was tied to the line, but before his neck could be tied to the bailer, the serpent put his head down the hole and started down it. The sand reel began

to unwind, and down Strickie went, headfirst, to the bottom of the well.

"Catch him! Stop him!" Gib cried. But it was too late. Strickie had reached the bottom.

"Take in the sand line!" Gib ordered. "Quick! Strickie will drown down there!"

Big Texas Toolie engaged the clutch. The sand line began to roll up on the sand wheel as Strickie was reeled up out of the well.

"Oh, that crazy snake!" cried Gib.

"What did he do that for?" shouted Toolie.

"I hope he didn't drown," said Gib anxiously.

When Strickie was drawn to the surface, Gib and Toolie ran to him with the first-aid kit. But that was not necessary. Strickie crawled to the sand pile and spit out the cuttings he had taken in his mouth.

"Look at that!" Gib exclaimed.

"Well, what do you know!" was all Toolie was able to say.

"Good old Strickie has made a bailer out of himself. He went down in the well headfirst, swallowed the cuttings down there, and now he has spit them out on the sand pile! I tell you, that Strickie is the most wonderful snake I ever saw. More wonderful than I could dream of even."

"Best bailer for takin' out sand I ever saw," Toolie agreed.

After that, Gib never used the metal bailer. Strickie had a bigger capacity than the bailer. And he seemed to like going down the well headfirst.

As long as Gib worked with Strickie, he never had to make another fishing tool, and he never had any trouble with fishing operations. Strickie liked to go down and bring up lost tools in his mouth.

Gib had good luck with the well. He struck a good flow of oil at 10,000 feet plus nineteen and nine-tenths blocks. Strickie's twenty-block length had just been enough added length to the 10,000-foot line.

12

The Self-Drilling Well

ONE TIME Gib started a well in South America that was about as unusual a well as a driller is ever likely to drill.

The location was in a valley, next to a rubber plantation. Soon the new rig was in operation, but the rope began to break. Gib spliced it, but it was no good. The rope was rotten and could not be used.

Gib dug to a depth of twenty blocks with Strickie. When he reached that depth he thought he would have to stop drilling. To make matters worse, Strickie began to have a strange look about him. He seemed pale.

Gib dosed him with quinine and rubbed him with Venango County crude oil liniment. It didn't seem to do much good. "Let's see if he's got a fever. I'll take his pulse." He felt the reptile's brow. "Temperature's normal. Pulse is O.K.," he mused.

Strickie sighed a deep sigh and wiggled off into the forest.

In a few hours he came back. Gib was surprised at his looks.
"He's got a good color now. Bright, clear, green. I wonder what
happened." Strickie seemed lively and he was his pleasant, good-
natured self.

The tragedy of a dry well became important again now that
the tragedy of Strickie's illness was gone.

Strickie kept moving back and forth between the rig and
the forest, pausing to look wistfully at Gib.

"By George," said Gib suddenly. "I think that snake is trying
to tell me something. I'll bet he wants me to go with him."

He joined the snake. The creature smiled happily and
squirmed his way into the woods, with Gib and Toolie at his
side. Strickie paused. Gib looked down. A strange substance
lay in the deep, cool shade. Gib stooped and touched it, puzzled.
Strickie squirmed happily and wiggled his tail. The oil driller
stood up and scratched his head as an aid to thought and to
help find words. The only words he found were not helpful
to Toolie. "I'll be doggoned," was all he could say.

"What is it?" Toolie asked.

"It's a snake skin, that's what it is. Strickie has shed his skin.
He has a nice new skin. This one stretched out here on the
ground is his old one," Gib explained.

Strickie took the old skin in his mouth and wiggled his way
back to the derrick, as Gib, still scratching his head, followed.
His thoughts were not yet complete. Gradually he came to
understand what was happening. "That snake is telling me to

use the old skin for a drilling line."

The old snake skin was tied onto Strickie and the drill began to sing once again. But there was to be a new problem, even though they were soon down to forty blocks—twenty blocks of Strickie and twenty blocks of the old snake skin.

It looked as though the drilling was going to have to stop. Gib didn't like that. He didn't like to fail. He was a winner, not a loser.

But there was no more drilling line. Before he gave the order to close down the job, a strange thing happened. The snake skin cable went slack. Then it tightened. Then it went slack again.

"What's wrong here? Man and boy, I have been a driller and I never saw such a thing before," Gib said.

If Gib was puzzled, Strickie was not. The tough snake skin broke away from the tools far below the surface. Strickie wiggled away to safety.

Gib heard the sound of the drill hammering away against the bottom. He knew it was rising and falling. Why? How?

"This well seems to be drilling itself," Gib said, unable to hide his disbelief.

"Them tools seem to be bouncin' up and down without no help from the rig," said Toolie. "But that ain't possible."

"It may not seem possible, but it's true! The tools are bouncing up and down," Gib declared.

"Let's get out of here!" Toolie shouted.

"No. Wait. Now I know what it is," Gib said.

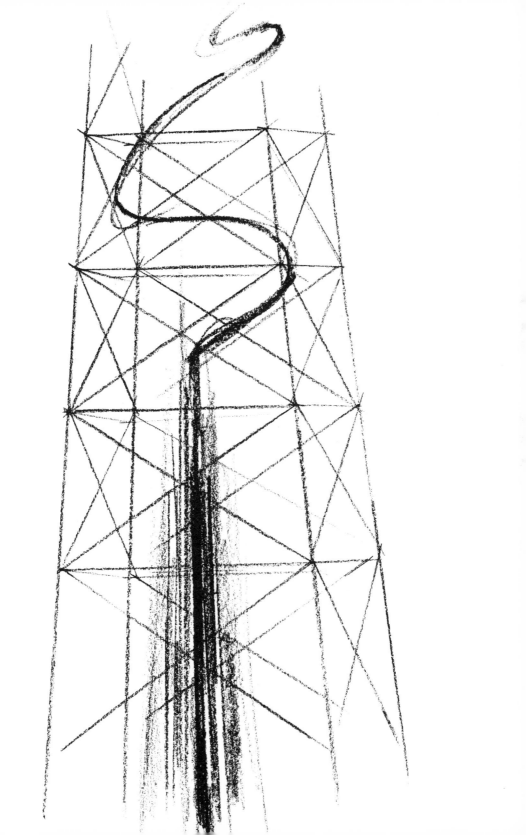

"What?" Toolie asked as he edged away.

"We have struck a vein of rubber. When the drill hits the bottom, it bounces back, higher each time. And the drill keeps on going and the hole gets deeper."

"That couldn't be," Toolie announced.

"Yes, it could be, and it's simple when you stop to think on it. There is a rubber plantation here. They take rubber from trees, but it has to come from some place. Naturally, the roots bring it up out of the ground. We must have hit the rubber down below," said Gib.

Now the string of tools was bouncing as high as the crown block before it dropped down into the hole.

Gib wondered how high it would bounce and if it would ever stop bouncing. Soon it was bouncing so high that he had time to eat a sandwich between the time it jumped up and the time it came down again.

Suddenly the drill bit didn't bounce as high. "I'll bet we went through the rubber vein," he cried.

The next time the drill came up, he struck it with a sledge hammer and pushed it aside. The bouncing bit went off at an angle and soared away over the hills like a meteor. They never saw it again.

Gib and Big Texas Toolie stood in silence, glad the excitement was over. They held their breaths and bent their ears over the hole. Deep down in the earth they heard a rushing, bubbling noise.

The master rope choker knew what it was. He had heard the sound before. "It's oil! We have struck oil!" he cried.

It was a fine, free flow of petroleum. It was the easiest and cheapest well Gib Morgan had ever brought in.

When Gib left South America and returned to the United States, he left Strickie well provided for. The buttermilk well was flowing strong, so the snake would always have a good supply of his favorite drink. Strickie is probably living there to this day, as contented and well fed as a smart boa constrictor should be.

Gib is still hard at work. There are oil fields all over the world. He is in one of them. It is probably a new field, a field that has not yet been proven, where the rig has not been stained by oil.

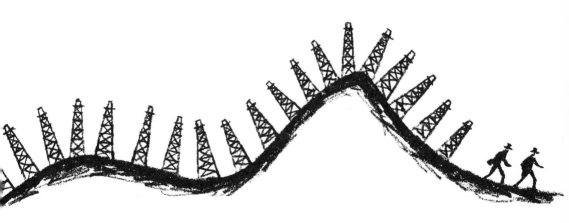

You can easily find the rig. It will be in the frozen, wind-swept arctic or it might be in a jungle or swamp. But then again, it could be in an ocean, or a lake, or in a hidden bay, or possibly it is a lonely tower in a desert, or is in a pleasant farm community. You can never be real sure about such things, because as everyone knows, oil is where you find it. But wherever it is, that's where Gib Morgan is. And Texas Toolie will be right there with him.

After you locate the field, it will be easy to find Gib. Just ask for the best driller, the one who tells the yarns.

The Author

HAROLD W. FELTON, a lawyer by profession, is an author known for his tall tales and his biographies for young readers. A long-time interest in American folklore led to his first book, an anthology of legends about Paul Bunyan. Since that time he has pursued folk heroes and tall tales with enthusiasm. His stories about Pecos Bill, John Henry, Fire-Fightin' Mose, Bowleg Bill, Mike Fink, and Sergeant O'Keefe rank him as a master yarn-spinner.

Mr. Felton was born in the Midwest, but has long been a resident of New York City. He and his wife now have a home in Falls Village, Connecticut, where he devotes his leisure time to writing for young people.

The Illustrator

PAUL SAGSOORIAN was born in New York and studied art at several art schools in New York City. He also went to the Map Making School of the U. S. Army. As a free-lance artist he does work for art studios and advertising agencies, as well as illustrations for books. In 1957 the American Institute of Graphic Arts selected a book illustrated by Mr. Sagsoorian as one of the Fifty Best Books of the Year.